The Adventures of Dusty Sourdough

by Glen Guy

THE ALASKA WILDERNESS SERIES — BOOK 4

IN THE ADVENTURE

F.I.R.E

PUBLISHED BY

O.A.T

OLD ALASKA TODAY — WASILLA, ALASKA

ISBN 1-59433-006-9

Library of Congress Catalog Card Number: 2003112677

This is a work of fiction, based on actual Alaska events of the 1800s. Many of the characters appearing in the Adventures of Dusty Sourdough were real, and some of the incidents actually took place. But the reader should be aware that, in the developing of characters and events, fictional literary license has been employed. While some of the characters and events herein are purely the creation of the author, every effort has been made to portray them with accuracy. However, the inherent dangers of the wilderness are real, sufficient unto themselves, and seldom has it been necessary to enhance their reality.

Photography by Décor Photo, Wasilla, Alaska,
Anchorage Museum of History and Art,
Sandy Guy, Lois J. Swensen, and Pudget Sound Museum.

Manufactured in the United States of America.

≈ DEDICATION ≈

*D*edicated in memory of the silver screen cowboys—my childhood heroes.

≈ ACKOWLEDGEMENTS ≈

*I*f it wasn't for you, my fans and friends, there wouldn't be any reason for writing; so first and foremost I must thank you for your loyalty and patience.

Thanks also to the support and help from everyone at Publication Consultants in bringing this work to fruition.

I must never forget the one with the most patience, my wife Sandy, the real Aura Lee in my life. She had to put up with me through all the ups and downs of writing, and she still came out on the other side loving me.

Books by Glen Guy

A Gift for Dusty

The Trail to Wrangell

Gold

Fire

❧ FOREWORD ❧

Larry Kaniut
Author of *Alaska Bear Tales*

Dusty Sourdough—he's a cross between a buckskin fringed Daniel Boone and the flashy Rhinestone cowboy a hundred years later. Dusty wears a hog leg on one hip and an 'Arkansas toothpick' Bowie knife in his belt. If you met Dusty on the street, you'd think you were in the wrong century. That's the Dusty Sourdough I know.

It was a long time after meeting Dusty before I learned that he had another name. This entertainer is the proverbial storyteller and troubadour. His real name is Glen Guy. But if you ever meet Dusty, you'll learn from the get go to love him—and you'll discover that Dusty fits him better than Glen. He's a throwback to way earlier times.

If you liked Louis L'Amour's Hondo, you'll love Dusty Sourdough. This rugged, take-no-prisoners, no nonsense former lawman came to Alaska in the 1800s, bringing his frontier justice and sense of morality with him. He was a man of character, principle, and good judgment, accustomed to taking on problems head on, and destined to overcome all odds.

Glen captured Dusty's 'doin's in his earlier books featuring the *Adventures of Dusty Sourdough: A Gift for Dusty*, *Trail to Wrangell* and *Adventure Gold*. Now he takes us a step beyond Dusty's earlier adventures with Alaska's brutal and mysterious environment involving wayward grizzlies, cold waters, and various mishaps to a time when a gold camp near Anchorage was thriving with good, but evil was trying to gain a foothold.

In many ways, the Alaska Dusty faced in the 1800s was no different from Alaska in this century—men came to get rich and/or to escape the long hand of the law. Men still leave all but their histories behind and hearken to the magical land of Alaska for the anonymity of The Last Frontier and her open arms, offering a new start and other riches.

In Dusty's (Glen's) new book, *Fire,* the story features the arrival of his friend Captain Dynamite Johnny O'Brien. Before you know it, Dusty takes on another challenge. With his trusty dog Shadow Spirit and his wife Aura Lee supporting him, and representing all a man could hope for, Dusty draws us into the newest thread of adventure. Using foreshadowing Glen warns the reader of the bad guys ahead, and the drama intensifies until the reader wants more of the good guy and can hardly wait for another Dusty Sourdough Adventure.

⫷ CHAPTER I ⫸

*L*ying in deep mud, he could feel small rivulets of sweat running down his gritty forehead and into his eyes. He didn't dare reach to wipe them, for if he did he was a goner. His heart was beating so loudly he was sure if the enemy came any closer, they too would hear it. He could hear them all around him, searching through the ankle-deep rotten vegetation. The stench and unbearable humidity in this Godforsaken swamp, might very well be his demise.

The captain had sent him into this snake-infested swamp to find a way around it, but instead of finding a better route, unfortunately, he'd found Johnny Reb. Now, in less than a moment they'd be all over him and capture was imminent. He would probably be killed on the spot, or taken to Andersonville, to spend the rest of the war rotting away in their stinking prison.

He could now hear every word they spoke and he knew he was had; he was at the end of his road.

"I know'd I saw a blue-belly, he's around here somewhere, just keep a-lookin'," ordered the burly, unshaven rebel sergeant.

"Iffin he gets away, I'll have yer hides."

It wasn't but a moment later when a young voice, filled with fear and excitement, shouted, "Here he is, I got him, I got him!"

The cold hand of fear gripped Dusty's heart as the young rebel's hand reached down and grabbed his arm. They had him. He fought and struggled but it was all in vain. There were too many and he was too exhausted to put up much of a fight. The rebel sergeant immediately pulled his pistol, laid it to Dusty's head, and cocked the hammer back ...

"Dusty ... Dusty wake up! Oh, please wake up, you're having another one of those terrible nightmares!" Aura Lee cried.

Dusty woke up wide-eyed in a cold sweat and realized it had happened again. "I'm sorry sweetheart," he said, with pain and regret in his voice, trying to joke it off. "I guess I shouldn't a had that there last slice of dried apple pie a fer we went ta bed. Ma always said eatin' before goin' ta bed could cause nightmares. I ... I sure didn't mean ta scare ya," he said sheepishly.

In truth, Dusty was never sure what brought on the bad dreams, but whatever it was, they seemed so real he often woke up drenched in sweat.

As usual, Dusty couldn't go back to sleep, so the next words to come out of his mouth were no surprise to Aura Lee.

"It's almost daybreak. I think I'll go down ta the kitchen and get a fire goin' in the cookstove and boil some coffee. I have a lot ta do today, what with Johnny Dynamite due up from Seattle anytime now since the ice is clearing out of the arm." Dusty leaned over and kissed Aura Lee gently, then slid out of bed and headed down the stairs.

Breakup was over and spring was upon the land. Alaska was gaining more daylight each day; however, it was still dark in the wee hours of the morning so Dusty lit the oil lamp at the bottom of the stairs, and headed into the kitchen. His faithful wolf dog Shadow Spirit looked up from the braided rug in front of the cookstove. She cocked her noble head and had a quizzical look on her face. Shadow Spirit was surprised to see her master in the kitchen so early. Usually Aura Lee was the first to rouse her from her comfortable spot in front of the stove.

'Well, a good mornin' ta ya, girl. How about you and me getting an early start on the day? Maybe if we get all our chores done, we'll mosey down ta the river and do a little gold-panning. Ya never know ... this might be the day we get lucky."

"By the way, yer ole friend, Johnny Dynamite, is due in any day now. That means everything around here will come to a halt ta celebrate the arrival of the first boat ta come up from Seattle since last fall. I reckon the women will put on a potluck and we'll all get together over at George's place. After supper, we'll get all the news about what's been goin' on down south."

As Dusty sliced bacon into the iron skillet he'd taken down from a hook in the ceiling he kept a running, one-sided conversation going with Shadow Spirit. The wolf dog always seemed to be listening intently, almost like she understood every word Dusty spoke.

When the bacon was done, Dusty went to the breadbox, found a fresh loaf of bread Aura Lee had baked the day before, and cut himself off a hearty slice. Warming it on the cookstove, then spreading a liberal dollop of wild-berry jam on it, he sat down at the kitchen table to enjoy his efforts and to ponder the day lying before him.

Winter had loosened its icy grip on Alaska, and now Mother Nature was budding out in all her glory. This signaled the ongoing cycle of life in the far North.

The men, eager to resume their search for riches

at their claims, knew full well their time would have to be divided between looking for gold and preparing for the coming winter, which always seemed to come much too fast.

Dusty wasn't any different from the other men in town and after a brief thought to his close call last summer when he'd inadvertently been sucked under and became trapped in an underground cavern, his thoughts returned to the

Décor Photo, Wasilla, Alaska

gold he discovered in the seams of his pockets and possible bag.

"Shadow Spirit, if we could figure a way back down into that underground cavern I got myself trapped in last summer, that is, without killin' ourselves, I bet we could find enough gold ta last us the rest of our born days."

The wolf dog's tail wagged and her eyes

sparkled as Dusty spoke to her. The bond between the two ran deep and already the stories told about the two around campfires had made them a legend in the north country. Tossing a crust to Shadow Spirit, Dusty got to his feet and took his plate to the sink, continuing to ponder the solution to accessing the underground cavern.

"I'll get my rifle, then you an' me will head down the arm and see if there's any sign of Johnny on the horizon. Maybe along the way we'll get a couple of rabbits for dinner."

Décor Photo, Wasilla, Alaska

In the shaded spots along the trail some snow remained, but it was disappearing fast and in its place little sprouts of green were starting to push through. This was a trail well used by Natives and settlers alike so it wasn't unusual to meet someone along the way. Dusty was pleasantly surprised to round a bend and see his good friend Walker sitting motionless on a big granite rock. At first Walker didn't acknowledge Dusty and Shadow

Spirit as they approached, but Dusty knew the Indian was aware of their presence and had probably known of their approach long before they appeared on the trail.

"Good morning, my friend," the Native spoke softly with perfect diction. He neither turned his head nor moved his body; for a moment it made Dusty wonder if he had even spoken the salutation at all.

Walker, an Athabaskan Indian, had befriended Dusty after he'd had an almost fatal run-in with a grizzly in a high mountain cave. By anyone's standards Walker was a giant. He was the biggest man Dusty had ever seen. He towered well over six feet eight inches, probably weighed in the neighborhood of three hundred pounds, and not an ounce of it was fat. The lines on his face were deceiving; they made it almost impossible to determine his age, but Dusty guessed it was somewhere in the mid-thirties. When he spoke, the words were those of a man with wisdom far beyond his years, and surprisingly he spoke in perfect English. He was a good teacher of this place called Alaska, and Dusty always listened carefully when Walker had something to say.

"Howdy," Dusty greeted, as he sat down near his

friend on the big rock. It was several minutes before either spoke another word. It was like that between the two friends; they respected the other's thoughts and solitude and waited for the other to finish his train of thought before striking up a conversation.

"Many moose this year," Walker said softly, breaking the silence. "Your caches will be full and food will be plentiful. I hope you and your friends will hunt wisely, not wasting what has been given to you. I have watched some of the new ones

Décor Photo, Wasilla, Alaska

who come looking for gold, and they sadden my heart. They have no concern for Mother Earth or for the animals put here for our use."

Dusty's voice betrayed deep sadness. "This I know, my friend. If we don't take care how we hunt and use this great land we will be the lesser for it and in the end it will be our loss. This land called Alaska is truly going to be the *last frontier* and we must take care of it."

Dusty and his friend sat silently for several minutes before Walker rose from his cross-legged position and bid farewell with a smile. As the Indian disappeared into the dense woods it was almost as if he had never been there. If Dusty hadn't known better, it would have been hard to believe anyone had shared this spot.

Dusty stood looking out across the beautiful waters of the Turnagain Arm pondering the words of his good friend Walker. He knew in his heart the wise Indian, much to his chagrin, had spoken the truth.

Dusty and Shadow Spirit reached Gull Rock close to lunchtime and decided to noon there. At this point of land one could on a clear day see all the way to Fire Island located at the mouth of the arm. Here, Dusty and Shadow Spirit could take lunch and at the same time

Lois J. Svensen

watch for their friend, Captain O'Brien.

After a cold but satisfying meal of moose jerky, Johnnycakes, and wild berries, the great white wolf dog and her master stretched out on a giant, flat rock jutting out over the water, and were soon fast asleep.

Dusty awoke an hour later at the sound of the excited but happy barking of Shadow Spirit as she danced around the rock. Looking in the direction she was focusing her attention on he could see nothing but empty, open water.

"What in tarnation are ya barkin' at? I can't see a thing." Reaching into his pack he pulled out his old brass telescope and looked toward Fire Island. "Well, I'll be. How did ya see that boat comin' around Fire Island? Iffin I'm not mistaken, that's Johnny's *Utopia*."

The *Utopia* was a single-stack coastal steamer with unmistakable lines, painted white and trimmed with red. She made way at about twelve knots and even fully loaded she drafted very little water.

Born in Ireland in 1851, Captain O'Brien had spent most of his life at sea, starting at the age of sixteen, when he was shanghaied on his way home from England. Until then, he'd enjoyed a pretty normal childhood. His career spanned the seven seas and his life was filled with adventure. He was perhaps the most knowledgeable sea captain of Alaska waters.

"Come on girl, let's get on back ta town and let 'em know Johnny will be along directly."

As Dusty and Shadow Spirit trotted off down the trail at a fast pace, Dusty was hoping to reach the

town ahead of the *Utopia* and knew he probably could at the pace he and the great wolf dog were traveling. As Dusty jogged down the trail his mind drifted back to last spring and all the trouble that had come with it …

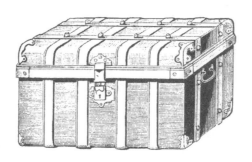

∼ CHAPTER 2 ∼

"*A*ll right men, step lively!" the jaunty little sea captain shouted over the sound of the ship's engine and the wind howling through its riggings. "We have a slack tide and should be in Hope by noon, just in time for some real grub at V. O. Rollie's place."

As the *Utopia* rounded Fire Island and headed up the Turnagain Arm, the captain went below to his cabin to make ready for port. He first put on his best uniform and made sure his cabin was in order. He checked the small fold-down desk that served him not only for ship's business, but also as his reading table and even a dining table when he wished to dine alone. It took him only a moment to find what he was looking for, and reaching down, he picked up a large manila envelope addressed to Dusty Sourdough. He had to admit, this letter, with a return address of Washington D.C., had his curiosity peaked. Who in Washington would know Dusty and what could this possibly be about? Captain O'Brien turned the letter over in his callused hands a couple of times and then slipped it inside his double-breasted sea captain's tunic, hoping his curiosity would soon be appeased. A rustling sound on his bunk caught his attention and he turned to pet his little friend. 'Well, you know, young lady, you'll soon be at your new home with a loving new master. I have one in mind—I only hope she will accept you." He smiled with a twinkle in his eye, picked up the little ball of fur, and headed topside.

The tide was turning as the *Utopia* approached the brand-new dock at Hope. This would be the first full summer it could be used. With the coming of the first ship of spring the whole town was at the dock to greet it. All were in a festive mood because this boat was bringing the first news anyone had heard from home since last fall, before they all became ice bound.

As the town folks watched the docking, it looked like total confusion to them, but in truth, it was organized and performed like a well-choreographed and rehearsed play. Some of the deckhands made ready with lines and others had started unlashing deck cargo to be offloaded as soon as the ship was secured to the dock. As the fore and aft lines were secured to the cleats on the dock, the gangway was lowered and a huge canvas bag with the letters U.S. MAIL stenciled 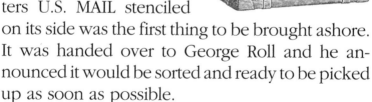 on its side was the first thing to be brought ashore. It was handed over to George Roll and he announced it would be sorted and ready to be picked up as soon as possible.

Next came the passengers, and as they stepped briskly down the gangplank Dusty scrutinized each one with a lawman's eye. Old habits died hard, and it had become a reflex. He had made a great effort to get back to town, barely making it in time to watch the new people step down the gangway. Something inside him told him it was important to be there to watch this event. Most of the passengers were typical of the gold rush fortune hunters. Many had spent their last nickel on passage and a meager outfit. Then there were the few others who, for whatever reason, had an air of wealth about them, and this made Dusty wonder why these types would risk life and limb when they already had more money than most. Dusty knew there was a thread, a common bond between the rich and poor ... it was called gold fever!

Each had a look of wonder and excitement and it took a practiced eye to see one other element lurking just below all the forced laughter and friendly bantering. Dusty could see it, and he knew it was the fear of the unknown. Some, too, had come with larceny in their hearts and had no intentions of looking for gold. They weren't about to spend sixteen to eighteen hours a day working a claim that might not even produce enough gold for a plate of beans at V.O. Rollie's grub tent. These were the card sharks, the con men, the thieves, and the claim jumpers ... the ones Dusty was on the lookout for, and to his chagrin he wasn't disappointed. Before long he had spotted the inevitable. Some bad news—they always showed up. Why should Alaska be different?

A tall, mean-looking man was standing at the rail next to the gangway and was looking the town over with cruel, hard eyes. His eyebrows were knitted together in intense concentration as he studied each face near the dock. His mouth had a cruel set to it as if he had never learned to smile. He stood six feet or better and was on the lean side, but still looked like he could handle himself. He wore the clothes of a cowboy and had a Colt strapped down low on his left hip with the butt facing forward for a cross-draw. On the opposite side he carried a bowie knife in a beaded sheath. The handle on the knife and the grips on his six-shooter showed plenty of use. As Dusty scrutinized him, the stranger must have felt eyes watching him because he turned and looked right into Dusty's eyes. They stared at each other for a moment and then the stranger turned abruptly and started for the gangway. Dusty didn't like the looks of this stranger, not one bit. He'd seen men just like this one in other gold camps and it had always turned out the same. He knew in his heart this time would be no different.

The excitement on the dock was contagious. Everyone was starved for information from home and as the soon-to-be neighbors stepped from the gangway they were swarmed upon like long-lost friends. In the excitement Dusty didn't see the stranger slip away.

Dusty was so deep in thought about the hard case he had spotted, as well as about a few others he had seen stepping down the gangplank, that he didn't feel Aura Lee slip up alongside him and was startled when she slipped her hand in his.

"Hey," she said, "where are you? You were so deep in thought you didn't hear Johnny call to you or even hear me come up behind you. What would people think if they knew the legendary Dusty Sourdough could have someone sneak up on him so easily?" She loved poking fun at her husband and laughed along with Dusty at her cleverness. Her wit was only one of the many things Dusty loved about her and he never took her joking personally.

Coming down the gangway, Johnny Dynamite spotted Dusty and was yelling at him when the lovely Aura Lee slipped up beside him.

The little ball of fur the captain had secretly tucked away made a noticeable lump in the front of his coat as he approached his two friends. Reaching out with one hand and holding his coat closed with the other, he warmly greeted his friend Dusty, and then, with a twinkle in his eye, he turned to Aura Lee saying; "And good day ma'am! I hope this day finds you well and in good spirits."

Aura Lee wondered why the captain was acting so formally, it wasn't like him, and it peaked her curiosity.

"Back in Seattle, just as we were preparing to cast off," he said, "I heard this noise and saw a flash of white running down  the dock toward the gangway, and before anyone could stop it ... well, she was on board and we were underway—and too late to do anything about it." About then, Johnny started stuttering, and what he was trying to say became academic. The subject of his agony pushed her little black nose out from between the highly polished brass buttons of his uniform coat and began licking at his hand. He couldn't contain her any longer and with a joyous bark the little furry white puppy leaped free from the confines of the captain's coat.

Aura Lee, purely by natural reflex, caught her before she could hit the ground and laughingly she asked the wiggling little ball of fur, "Where are you going? You look like a little white bear cub, and look at that busy little pink tongue! Why, you're so cute I could squeeze the stuffin' right out of you!"

The puppy was licking and wiggling with uncontrollable excitement as Dusty tried to ask her, "What in the world has Johnny brought to you? It does look like a little bear cub!"

"Oh, isn't she cute!" Aura Lee cried with joy. "Can I keep her? Aura Lee pleaded.

Dusty could hear the joy in her voice as she spoke of the little critter and just like all the other times, he could never refuse her the desires of her heart and said, "Well, if ya really want the little critter, who am I ta say no ... I just wonder how Shadow Spirit and Dog'll get along with her. They're both pretty set in their ways ..."

Décor Photo, Wasilla, Alaska

"They'll get along fine," Aura Lee interrupted as she held the puppy down for Shadow Spirit to sniff. "Look at Shadow Spirit, her tail's wagging and she has a smile on her face." In truth, Shadow Spirit wasn't too sure exactly what was going on, but she did know that Aura Lee was holding a baby of her own kind and that was all she needed for her mothering instincts to take over as she sniffed and licked the new family member.

"It looks like you've got a new addition to your family." Johnny Dynamite said as Shadow Spirit gently licked the little furry puppy. "What are ya goin' ta call her?"

Unwittingly Dusty had already given her a name and didn't even know it, but Aura Lee answered immediately.

"We'll call her Little Bear," Aura Lee said with confidence. "After all, Dusty said she looked like a little bear ... look at her, I bet she's as brave as a bear too!"

Little did Aura Lee know how true her prophecy of Little Bear's tenacity would come to pass ...

With a big smile you couldn't wipe off Aura Lee's face, she thanked the beaming sea captain and said she had to get back to the cabin to start preparing supper. She bid her good-bye and started walking away. Realizing in that instant she had forgotten to ask the captain to dinner, she turned and said, "You will be taking your evening meal with us, won't you, Captain?" She said it more as a statement of fact than as a question, and of course, he graciously accepted.

The salty sea captain had become close friends with Dusty and Aura Lee and cherished the little time he could spend with them on his trips to Hope. In melancholy moments he wished he had chosen another life besides the sea, but usually the feeling would pass when he realized the sea was his life and his love. He knew he could never be happy bound to land, knowing the rolling sea was beckoning him to another adventure.

As Dusty and Johnny walked down the dock toward town they were too busy talking to notice Shadow Spirit's anxiety. Her hackles were up and she emitted an almost inaudible whine. But all this, unfortunately, went unnoticed by her master.

By the time the two friends reached George Roll's store on Main Street, a crowd had already started to gather and was waiting with anticipation for the storekeeper to get the mail sorted and handed out. Realizing what the commotion was all about reminded Johnny of the special envelope from Washington D. C. he had inside his coat for Dusty.

"Say," he said. "I almost forgot about this." He

reached inside his coat and pulled out the envelope that had aroused his curiosity. Handing it to Dusty, he said, "Just before I sailed, this feller came running up the gangway in a huff. He asked me where I was bound. When I told him, he asked if I knew you. I told him I did and that's when he handed me that there envelope. He was a mysterious sort of guy with a no-funny-business air of authority about him. He said to make sure you got it directly and not to show it to anyone, then he turned and walked away without another word. Now if that don't get a man's curiosity up, I don't know what would!"

Dusty could tell Johnny wanted him to open the envelope right then, but when he heard how the letter was delivered and saw the return address, he folded it carefully and slipped it into his pocket.

"Ain't ya even gonna read it?" Johnny blurted out in frustration. "It—it looks mighty important."

Dusty just smiled at his friend and said, "It can wait," and headed into the store.

The store was crowded so Dusty went right to the shelf where George stocked different calibers of ammunition and took down a tin containing the caliber that fit his Winchester.

Turning to walk over to the counter to pay for his purchase, he felt someone watching him. Looking about the store he could see no one was paying any attention to him. Still he felt uneasy. It was a feeling he never ignored.

"Howdy, Mrs. Roll!" Dusty greeted as he reached into his pocket for money.

"That'll be four bits," she said with a big smile. "Dusty ... Dusty! Did you hear me?"

As Dusty stepped up to the counter to pay, he noticed a reflection in the glass front of the display case behind Mrs. Roll and for a brief moment he froze, as the hairs on the back of his neck stood up.

"I ... I'm sorry Ma'am. I must be daydreaming," he said, trying to cover the bad feeling he had gotten, as the face disappeared when he turned to look out the front window.

"You look like you just saw a ghost!" the storekeeper's wife declared.

☞ CHAPTER 3 ☞

*T*he dandy didn't like the suspicious looks he'd got from the grizzled man on the dock and when he saw him a second time through the window of the general store, he knew, without a doubt, this guy could cause him some grief.

Watching from across the street he waited until the suspicious stranger left the store, then strolled over, pushed his way through the crowd outside, and entered the building. He spotted what he was looking for but he didn't walk toward it or even give it a second glance. He walked up to the counter and asked where the saloon was. To his dismay he was told by the lady smiling at him that he would have to go to Sunrise, because whiskey and gambling weren't allowed in Hope. After asking where he could buy a horse, he headed up the street to the small livery stable the lady had directed him to.

Few horses were kept in Alaska because it was hard to winter them. Mules were the beast of burden of choice because they were sturdy, sure-footed, and more adaptable to the rugged terrain of Alaska than a horse. Feed had to be shipped up by boat, and so did bedding straw and other supplies. This raised the overhead of a livery stable sky-high and unfortunately the expense had to be passed on to the unhappy customer.

"Howdy!" the dandy greeted the stable owner.

"Yeah, what can I do fer ya? I don't have any fancy carriages and only four horses" the bowlegged old horse wrangler said with a skeptical, appraising look.

"Well, what do you have to ride?" the shady-looking man asked, trying to sound tough, with unmistakable anger and contempt in his voice.

"One of them horses might do, not the best ridin' stock, but it beats walkin'," he said with a chuckle and a twinkle in his eye.

"If that's all you have, I guess I don't have a choice, do I? How much?"

Without hesitating the stableman said, "A hundred fifty U.S."

The outraged look on the dandy's face caused the horse wrangler to take a step backward. The corners of the dude's mouth were curved down and his snakelike eyes had the cruelest look the old wrangler had ever seen, and he wouldn't soon forget it.

"That's robbery without a gun!" the dude fumed. "It's a nag!" He roared. For a moment the stable owner thought the dude was going for the six-gun that was slung low on his hip. Relief coursed through the old-timer when the dandy pulled out his wallet instead of a Colt.

"I guess I don't have much choice," he said as his voice calmed down, and a smile came to his lips, but didn't reach his eyes. He counted out his money and the stableman went out to the

Anchorage Museum of History and Art

corral and brought in a horse that stood a good fourteen hands tall.

"Here ya go," the wrangler said, handing him the lead rope.

"What about the saddle and bridle?" the dandy asked, starting to fume all over again.

Again the hostler stood his ground and said;

"What about em? ... Ya bought a horse, mister. Nothin' was said about a rig fer him. That'll cost ya 'nother fifty U.S."

This was the final straw! In one quick motion

the dandy had the startled cowboy by the front of his shirt and his feet jerked off the ground. He was about to slug him, when a voice as cold as a glacier spoke behind him.

"Are you as tough with everyone, or just ole men? ... Iffin I was you I'd put him down real gentle like."

There was something in the voice behind him that got his immediate attention and put a chill down his spine. The dandy knew whoever had happened upon them meant business. He loosened his grip and the old wrangler settled to the ground and took a step backward. Turning around, the would-be tough guy confronted the man behind the voice, who was standing just inside the stable's big front doors holding a Winchester in one hand, loosely pointed at him.

This new player wasn't a big man, not in stature anyway, but there was something about him that was all business. It felt like his ice-blue eyes were staring through him and the dandy knew he had made his first mistake in this new land.

⇔ CHAPTER 4 ⇔

As Aura Lee walked the trail back home with her new friend, Little Bear, scampering behind her, she stepped briskly down the trail with a joy in her heart and a song on her lips.

The sky was the bluest of blues and the song birds had returned and were singing their joyous songs of spring as Aura Lee moved along the trail humming her own little song. She stepped across a babbling stream no more than three feet wide and had thought nothing about it, that is, not until she heard a string of mournful yaps behind her. When she turned to see what the ruckus was about, she broke into uproarious laughter as her eyes fell on her new friend. Little Bear, who had been following at her heels, found the small stream a formidable barrier. Laughing so hard at the antics the puppy was using to get Aura Lee's attention, caused tears to start rolling down her cheeks as she stepped back across the stream to pick up the squirming little ball of fur. Immediately Little Bear showed her gratitude by giving Aura Lee a right proper face washing with a very busy little pink tongue. Laughing with delight, Aura Lee turned, stepped back across the stream, and resumed her walk home with the furry little ball held tight in her arms.

Captain O'Brien was more like family than a guest, but still she wanted everything to be just right when he came to dinner. Going into her pantry she took down vegetables she had put up (canned) from her last summer's garden and then gathered the makings for baking fresh bread. When she got the fire blazing in her cookstove she brought in from their root cellar a package of moose steaks still frozen hard as a rock. A friend had brought them by the day before. All the while she scurried about the kitchen Little Bear stayed right at her heels. When Aura Lee stopped for a moment and looked down at her, Little Bear looked up and gave the look only a puppy can give, causing Aura Lee to reach down and give her a loving pat. Already this irresistible little critter had the lady of the house wrapped around her little paw.

The day slipped by quickly and as the shadows of the afternoon grew longer Aura Lee began to wonder where Dusty had gotten off to. She thought he should have been home by now and was starting to get a little concerned. She knew trouble could pop up anywhere 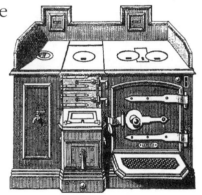 and usually where there was trouble Dusty was more than likely in the middle of it.

These thoughts brought back the scary memories of last summer but she realized she had no real reason to worry now, with the demise of that claim jumper named Jake. He was a wicked man and had been taken care of by the [1]Cannon Ball. Fortunately, almost all the gold he had stolen

[1]The Cannon Ball was a nickname given to the boar tide that ripped up the Turnagain Arm like a runaway freight train.

was recovered and things had soon returned to normal around the little town of Hope.

It was while trying to take her mind off these misgivings that she suddenly realized they had been with her since she watched the passengers on the *Utopia* step ashore earlier that morning. She was too perplexed to understand why this should cause concern. After all, this was always a time of celebration, not of worry. At that moment, Little Bear rose from her spot near Aura Lee's feet and started growling in the direction of the door. It surprised Aura Lee that this sweet little puppy could sound so aggressive, but she got the obvious message and moved quickly to the coat pegs by the door, where Dusty's Colt hung in a well-worn holster. She pulled the Colt from the holster and slowly lifted the latch and eased the door open. Cautiously, leading with the gun in her hand, she stepped out the door.

≈ CHAPTER 5 ≈

"*W*hat's goin' on around here?" Dusty asked with cold steel in his voice.

The dandy couldn't quite figure out who or what this interruption was, but as they stood there staring each other down, his confidence began to return.

"This ain't any business of yours and if you know

what's good for you you'll back out of here before I grab iron and blow a hole in you big enough to run that big, ugly nag back there through! You understand me?" The dandy thought he sounded pretty tough and he usually could intimidate anybody with his threatening mouth, but when he heard the metallic sound of a hammer being pulled back a cold chill went through him. His bluff was being called.

Dusty never blinked once as the dandy issued his ultimatum. As the man finished ranting, Dusty thumbed back the hammer on his Winchester and stood there with an unmistakable look on his face and it wasn't a look of fear. "Stranger," Dusty started, "you're lucky I showed up when I did!"

The dandy got a perplexed look and was having a hard time understanding how this guy showing up was lucky for him, when he was about to teach this stable trash a lesson in manners he wouldn't soon forget.

"Ole Jeb there," Dusty continued, "may seem on the outside ta be pretty defenseless, but you just don't know how close you were ta the edge."

"What do you mean, the edge?" the stranger interrupted. "I was about to teach that old fool a thing or two about who he was dealing with!"

"And just who is he dealing with?" Dusty asked sarcastically, in a menacing tone.

The dandy didn't like where this was leading and he liked this fellow with the Winchester even less.

With arrogance in his voice the stranger snarled, "I don't know who you are, and if you're not the law, I think this conversation is over!"

He turned to grab the lead rope of the horse and froze in his tracks. Standing right in front of him, blocking his way, was the man he had thought to be a spineless stable hand. But now he was holding an Arkansas toothpick. By the look on his face, he wasn't spineless, and he was ready to use that ugly-looking knife.

"Look, fellows," he said with a complete change in his demeanor. "Maybe I was a little hasty in my judgment." His voice quivered and beads of sweat started to form on his forehead as he started to back up. "I guess maybe things cost a lot ... I mean a little more up here at the end of the world than in say, California or, or Texas," he stammered.

"You guessed right, stranger!" Jeb spoke with fire in his eyes and authority in his voice. "And we don't take lightly around here ta any abuse or name callin'."

"Now I ain't agonna ask you again—what's your name, mister?" Dusty demanded with finality in his voice.

Turning sideways so as not to have his back to either man, the stranger said, "Blackjack, Blackjack Jones! My friends call me Blackie. I'm the greatest poker player this side of—of, anyplace," He stated smugly.

"Well, Mister Jones! You best be mindin' yer manners around here cause ya never know who you're a-dealin' with. Ole Jeb here, he's the best knife handler here 'bouts. He can skin out a runnin' grizz so fast, that bear will be halfway up the mountain a'fer he realizes he's done lost his hide. What I'm tryin' ta tell ya is, Jeb there was 'bout ta fillet you like a fresh salmon!"

Jones could hardly take his eyes off the menacing-looking knife held steady in Jeb's leather-worn hand. Without a word, he reached in his pocket and pulled out enough money to pay for the saddle. With shaking hands he mounted the horse, and with pure hate in his eyes Jones looked down at Dusty.

"We'll meet again," he said, with a threatening tone to his voice. He swung around and glared at the stable owner, turned, and rode off toward Sunrise without another word. He never looked back.

"I got a bad feelin' 'bout that stranger," Dusty said to himself in a barely audible voice.

After bidding good-bye to Jeb, Dusty decided it was too late in the day to get much hunting done and he knew Aura Lee would be starting to worry, so he started for home.

As he hit the trail home he realized he hadn't seen Shadow Spirit since the offloading of the *Utopia*. This didn't concern Dusty; he knew she could take care of herself, and she'd always been free to come and go as she pleased. He  was just curious, wondering what she was up to.

Dusty thought about the day's activities as he walked along the trail, enjoying the warmth of the afternoon sun, and he remembered the letter Dynamite O'Brien had hand-delivered. Reaching inside his shirt he pulled out the

envelope and tore it open. He unfolded the
letter and read:

UNITED STATES MARSHAL'S SERVICE

WASHINGTON D.C.

Dusty,
I hope this letter gets to you and
finds you in good health. Your
friendship and undying dedication
to the service are sorely missed.

By now you have probably realized
the lack of law and order in the far
North. As you know, I have never
been a man to mince words, so I'll
just get to it.

Some pretty unsavory characters
have disappeared from the land-
scape down here and we have reason
to believe they're headed your way.
Now I know you're saying, what's
this got to do with me? I know you're
retired, but you still hold your
commission and we desperately need
you back in the service. Before you
say no, read the rest of this letter.

Several months ago we started

noticing known members of the Ace Hawkins' gang starting to drift north toward Seattle. Six months ago, up in Idaho, Ace got caught cheating in a card game at a logging camp and was beat within an inch of his life and then thrown out of camp. Four days later the saloon and half the camp burned down under suspicious circumstances. The saloonkeeper, the one that caught Hawkins cheating, was found dead in the ashes.

We can't prove Hawkins set the fire or killed the saloonkeeper, but without a doubt, we know he did it. He was spotted a month later in Seattle and then we lost track of him again. The only thing we can figure is he'd hopped aboard one of the many boats headed to the goldfields in Alaska.

Dusty, this gang is bad news and we believe they're all headed your way. I know Alaska is a big place and they may not even show up where you are, but if they do, you'll be the only one who can stop them.

```
I'm sorry to ask you to do this as you
have served more than should be
expected of anyone, but please
please pin your badge back on ...

Your Friend,
Sam Tuckerman
United States Marshal
```

Dusty read the letter again, and then reached into the manila envelope and took out what looked to be wanted posters. The faces on the six posters were an unsavory lot, and they were wanted for a variety of charges, but the one that caught his eye was wanted for nothing—anyway, nothing that could be proven. This poster was not for public notice and was posted only between lawmen for their enlightenment. The name on the bottom wasn't familiar, Ace Hawkins, but the face was none other than Blackjack Jones!

∾ CHAPTER 6 ∾

*T*he horse's gait jarred every bone in Blackjack's body and with every jolt he fumed. He'd show those losers. "When I get through with them, they'll come beggin' for help 'cause I'll have all their money," he said to himself with a chuckle.

It was a short ride to Sunrise and when Blackjack arrived he saw a vast difference between this town and the one he had just left. Even at this early hour he could hear the sounds of the saloon's pianos and the loud voices of their patrons. This town was wide open and ripe for the pickin'; it was as

different from Hope as night is from day. Hope didn't allow gambling or saloons, whereas this one had at least three saloons and each one of them had gambling tables complete with the usual cardsharps. Black-jack looked up and down the muddy street of Sunrise and spotted one of the saloons called *The Sluice Box*. The sign also boasted the

friendliest dealers in town. Another sign hang-ing next to the saloon's swing doors read: Blackjack dealer wanted, must be honest and dependable, apply inside.

This was made to order, Blackjack thought to himself as he ripped the sign down, with an evil smile on his lips. He stepped into the noisy, smoke-filled saloon and let his eyes adjust to the dimness before moving toward the make-shift bar.

The *Sluice Box* was typical of mining camp saloons. The bar was made of rough-cut planks, already polished smooth by continual use, and was set atop two empty whiskey barrels. The tables were hand hewn, as were the chairs. The saloon itself was a combination of logs and canvas and had rough-cut planks for a floor. The interior was dimly lit by oil lanterns and what little light was able to come through the filthy front window.

"What can I do fer ya?" the barkeep asked in an unfriendly tone.

"I'm lookin' for the boss of this … this establishment. Would he be around?" Blackjack asked with obvious disdain in his voice.

"Snarlin' Sam's in the back sleepin' an he ain't wantin' ta be waked up!" the barkeep said with a sneer.

Blackjack had all the attitude he could take for one day and his temper boiled over. Suddenly, reaching across the makeshift bar with lighting speed, he grabbed the barkeep by the front of his filthy apron with one hand, and as if by magic, a Colt appeared in the other. Dragging the surprised man halfway across the bar, Blackjack shoved the Colt under his nose and asked with a snarl, "How'd you like a hole where that ugly nose is? You're about to have a real bad day unless you come up with a better answer." He shoved the Colt hard enough to start the barkeep's nose bleeding.

"I—I, I'm not supposed ta wake him up," the now scared and stuttering barkeep managed to say.

The tension in the saloon was thick. By now the group of miners had all but stopped what they were doing so they could watch as the drama played out before them. Almost everyone in town at one time or another had had a run-in with Big Mike, the barkeep, and he had left very few with a good taste in their mouths. He was bigger than most and he liked nothing better than to bully anyone smaller. More than once down in New Mexico, where he came from, he'd been in scrapes with the law, all because he got a little too exuberant with a club he always kept behind whatever bar he was working at the time. They figured whatever happened to him he deserved; they hadn't seen many people with the nerve to stand up to him like this stranger was and they were enjoying the turn of events. They were happy to see someone at last putting Big Mike in his

Anchorage Museum of History and Art

place. Little did they know the stranger they were admiring would soon make their bully of a bartender look like a saint.

"Don't make me ask you again, 'cause if I do, it'll be the last words you ever hear, understand!"

At that moment the unmistakable sound of someone pulling back the twin hammers of a double-barreled shotgun brought a dead silence to the saloon.

"Mister, I don't take favor ta someone roughin' up my barkeep, even if he probably does deserve it. Ya see, they're kinda hard ta find, what with every man jack here 'bouts out lookin' fer gold. So lessn' you want ta become a terrible mess ta clean up when this here Greener goes off, I'd advise ya ta turn loose of him and lay that there six-shooter on the bar."

Obviously by now Blackjack was coming to the conclusion he was having a real bad day and not wanting to make it any worse, he did as he was told. Turning ever so slowly, he faced his latest challenge.

Now, staring down the twin barrels of a 10-gauge Greener will take the starch out of most anybody and Blackjack wasn't any different from the next guy.

The man holding the sawed off Greener was plain ugly, with or without the shotgun, and Blackjack knew his grip on life was tenuous at best. This guy looked like something from a bad dream. Somewhere along his life's path something or someone had altered his natural looks considerably—and not for the better. He was a hulk of a man well over six-feet and his girth was enormous, his huge belly hung over whatever belt or gun belt he was wearing. It was obvious to Blackjack the man enjoyed his food and drink. His face was one only a mother could love. The whole left side was a mass of scars starting at what were the remains of an eyebrow. It was scraggly at best with a few unruly hairs shooting off in different directions. The strange thing about it, though, was how it was pulled up toward what used to be his hairline, which in reality didn't exist. His left cheek was a bright pink scar and his upper lip was pulled up in a permanent snarl. It was hard not to stare at him or to wonder what or who had done this to him.

"Take it easy," Blackjack said with as much authority as anyone could muster looking into a 10-gauge. "I came in here looking for a job and this worthless, good-for-nothing barkeep wouldn't let me talk to the owner. So I was in the process of changing his way of thinking, till you and that Greener interrupted our conversation."

"Well, stranger, me and this here Greener own *The Sluice Box*. People here 'bouts call me Snarlin' Sam and I don't much appreciate bein' woke up from my beauty nap by the likes of you or anybody else."

This brought a roar of laughter from the miners gathered around the excitement, until Snarlin' Sam turned and glared at them. His glare could stop an eight-day clock from ticking, so once again the room turned dead silent. Sam wasn't joking, even if it did sound funny. The glint in Sam's eyes spoke volumes of anger. Snarlin'

Sam turned and said, "Ya have a mighty strange way of askin' fer a job. What do ya do besides rough up barkeeps?"

Without a word, Blackjack grabbed the sign off the bar that he had ripped from the wall outside, and threw it at Snarlin' Sam's feet.

"I'm the best dealer you ever seen," he said with arrogance, "and I can make this—this establishment," he said with obvious disdain in his voice, "more money than you can count. They call me Blackjack, or friends call me Blackie."

"Well, Mr. Blackjack!" Sam snarled, "I don't need no trouble-makin', high-faultin', double-dealin' cardsharp around here. I expect my dealers ta be honest and friendly and the latter one you don't appear ta be. But I do need a dealer, so let's go back in my office and talk."

Blackjack turned to pick up his Colt and Sam growled, "leave it where it lays. It'll be safe till we're done talkin.' That is iffin what ya have ta say, I like!"

Blackjack followed Sam back to his office located behind the poker tables in the rear of the saloon. Blackie never missed much and he noticed a huge plate glass mirror covering most of the wall behind the poker tables. A slight, undetectable smile came to his lips. As Blackjack entered the boss's office, to his surprise, he found it to be quite nice. It had all the finery one would expect to find in the office of an eastern gentleman—carpet on the floor, oil-burning glass chandelier, huge mahogany desk, and a high-backed swivel chair. In one corner was a double bed, adorned with a feather-tick mattress. The wall dividing the office from the saloon was covered with massive, maroon velvet drapery and it was obvious to Blackie why this was. The mirror he had seen on his way in was two-way.

The moment the door closed behind the two men their un-friendly, rough demeanor changed to one of long-lost friends.

"Ace—or should I say Blackjack—you ole double-dealin' card shark. I'd of thought by now someone would've shot you fer dealin' off the bottom of the deck. Sorry fer the rough stuff out there, but I got a sweet thing goin' here and I didn't want anyone knowin' we knew each other."

Blackjack nodded.

"I'm fleecing these fools out of their gold as fast as they dig it up, said Sam. I had a little problem with my last dealer when he caught a case of honesty and threatened ta spill the beans on my

operation. Terrible thing happened ta him. One day he went fer a walk and never came back. A bear musta' got him." They both laughed. "I can use ya, Ace—I mean Blackjack."

"Some of the other boys are drifting up," Black-

jack said, "and we plan to clean this place out before they know what hit 'em; this place and Hope. There's a couple reprobates over there I intend to take care of personally. That fellow they call Dusty Sourdough and the old man running the stable. They both made a fool out of me and I'm fixing to make them pay. With their hides."

"I'd be real careful with your threats," Sam advised. "I don't know much about the old man at the livery, but that Dusty Sourdough isn't one to under-estimate. There's more to him than meets the eye. Word's around that he can track an ant across a rock pile, and has, for a fact, killed a grizzly with his bare hands. I do believe it'd take a heap of killin' ta put him under. The Natives here 'bouts believe him ta be somethin' special."

"Well, special or not, if he gets in my way again, we'll see how he handles a belly full of lead."

≈ CHAPTER 7 ≈

As Aura Lee eased out onto the porch, gun in hand, her new guardian had no such thoughts—she figured head-on was the only way to meet an unknown threat. With the toughest growl and bark a puppy her size could muster, she shot between Aura Lee's legs and headed into the woods. Little Bear was so fast it all happened before Aura Lee could grab her. Throwing caution to the wind, Aura Lee took hold of her skirts, and yelling at the top of her lungs she ran after the little ball of fur as swiftly as her feet could carry her.

Little Bear had taken the trail leading to the creek and was far ahead of Aura Lee by the time she

Décor Photo, Wasilla, Alaska

reached the small, but fast-moving stream. To her dismay as she sniffed around she found there were so many scents abounding about the surging water's bank, that she couldn't distinguish one from the other. She was sure the one she was following was that of a man, but here at the water's edge it had disappeared and in its place were all these other pungent smells her sensitive little nose couldn't identify. To a city dog the scents were unfamiliar, but some born, natural instinct told her to be wary, if not fearful of some of the unfamiliar smells.

Little Bear's sensitive ears heard Aura Lee long

before she came into sight. The bond between the two was already unshakable and Little Bear could tell by her master's voice she was very upset with her, but couldn't for the life of her understand why. Wasn't her natural instinct to protect her master correct?

"You foolish, brave little puppy," Aura Lee cried as she approached and picked up the wiggling ball of white fur. "It's much too dangerous for someone as small as you to go charging off into the woods alone. An eagle could swoop down and carry you away or any other number of critters would consider you a tasty meal."

Décor Photo, Wasilla, Alaska

By now Aura Lee's voice had softened and tears were beginning to run down her cheeks. Seeing this, Little Bear's pink tongue quickly began trying to dry the tears streaming from Aura Lee's eyes. Her voice softened even more as she said, "Oh, I can't stay mad at you for being so brave and charging out to protect me against something totally unknown to you."

Speaking the thought brought a sudden chill to her and in that moment a feeling of danger came over her and she sensed that danger was very near. "I don't know what you heard that got you so excited," she said, looking across the stream into the deep-dark forest. It was so dense anything or anyone could be hiding only a few yards away and it would be completely undetectable. She could feel eyes watching her and wasn't sure what her next move should be.

Décor Photo, Wasilla, Alaska

Nonchalantly, she pretended to look about trying to show as little interest as possible, even though she knew something was amiss and danger was near.

"Well," she said with as much lilt to her voice as possible, "we'd better get started back. You'll get used to all the new and strange noises we have around here, and believe you me, we have aplenty."

With that said in a voice she hoped was not too loud to sound unnatural, she turned and headed back up the trail toward home. To the casual eye this would have looked completely normal, except for one slight error ... She never put Little Bear down to run along behind. In truth, she was afraid the fearless little dog wouldn't back away from whatever was watching them.

The light was fading fast, but fortunately Aura Lee knew the trail well and navigating it in failing light presented very little difficulty. At a fast walk she should be able to reach the cabin before total darkness. She only hoped the special dinner she had left baking in the oven wasn't ruined, and more than that, she hoped whatever or whoever she  *Sandy Guy* was sure was watching her from the woods across the river, wouldn't try to follow or catch her ...

As Aura Lee moved quickly along the trail she couldn't help stopping every now and then to listen behind her for any sounds that would give away the presence of someone or something following close behind. To her surprise,

Little Bear's growl, which she felt more than she heard, because she still had the puppy in her arms, froze her in her tracks. Little Bear wasn't looking behind where she thought the danger to be, but to her surprise the dog's attention was directed up the trail in the direction they were traveling.

"Shhs!" Aura Lee whispered as she ducked off the trail into the alder brush and fireweed that skirted the trail. Ducking behind a large cottonwood she strained her ears to listen. She too heard the sounds of someone moving toward them on the trail—and whoever it was, was coming fast!

≈ CHAPTER 8 ≈

Dusty, sitting on a log beside the trail, reread-
ing the letter for a second time, was trying to
justify the thoughts and feelings going through
his mind. He had spent most of his adult life
serving his country as a United States marshal.
Now, even though his [2]resignation had never
been accepted, he was being asked to pin his
badge back on. Maybe if he hadn't found Aura

[2]*This is explained in book 3 "GOLD"*

Lee, fallen in love and married, the decision might have been easier to come by. This wasn't even taking into consideration his age. He was not a young man any longer. He'd planted roots and made lifelong friends in the growing community of Hope. For the first time in his life he was truly content and had no desire to leave any of this behind.

The marshal side of him knew Alaska needed civil law and lawmen to enforce it. Because of the gold discovery and more new finds happening practically every week, people were coming to Alaska by the thousands on any and all boats heading north. Unfortunately, not all were coming in search of gold via hard work—some came to swindle or steal it, and that's where a strong, no-nonsense lawman was needed.

Dusty was one such lawman—tough, but compassionate, and a man who didn't have an ounce of backup in him. Marshal Tuckerman knew this and he also knew of Dusty's fierce loyalty to the marshal's service. He was relying on this quality to be the driving force to push Dusty into pinning his badge back on.

Reading the letter, Dusty couldn't help thinking back on the day's incidents. Blackjack and the other hard cases he'd noticed coming down the gangway of the *Utopia* were, he had no doubt, some of the men mentioned in Tuckerman's letter. He had been a lawman long enough that it was like second nature to spot men who were less than honest. Maybe they weren't all part of one gang, but it didn't take long for their kind to meet up with each other. None of them, for the next few days, would be hard to find. They would all sooner or later migrate to Sunrise. Hope, being a dry community, would have nothing to offer their kind, but Sunrise, on the other hand, had three saloons and all the things going on that would attract them.

Dusty had already been involved in putting an end to a rash of claim jumping incidents, but he knew there were other ways of robbing a man of his hard-earned gold, that didn't involve a six-gun or violence.

"Come on, Shadow Spirit, we better get ourselves home ta see if we can help Aura Lee with anything 'afore the Captain gets there. I'll want ta ponder over this here letter some and talk it over with Aura Lee a mite, so no use thinkin' on it anymore now, I'm sure when the decision comes I'll be the first ta know," he said with a chuckle. He got to his feet and headed up the trail toward home with Shadow Spirit leading the way.

Dusty was a man of action and could make a

decision in a split second if the case need be, but when it was a call that could possibly affect him and Aura Lee for the rest of their lives, and he had control over it, he needed the time to think on it. He was sure he had plenty of time to do just that. Little did Dusty realize the

Décor Photo, Wasilla, Alaska

decision was already out of his control and it would be coming sooner than he thought, much sooner!

Shadow Spirit came to such a sudden stop at the edge of the clearing surrounding their cabin that Dusty almost fell over her. If her abrupt stop hadn't gotten Dusty's attention, her raised hackles and the low growl coming from deep within her chest certainly did.

"Easy, girl," Dusty said in almost a whisper. "I see it too." He eyed the cabin door ajar. Aura Lee would never leave the door open, what with all the wild critters about, not to mention mosquitoes and the likes. She was always on him to close the door behind himself.

Backing ever so slowly into the shadows of the forest, Dusty and the great white wolf dog started to circle so they could approach the cabin from the side without windows.

To someone who had the rare opportunity to watch Shadow Spirit and Dusty work together, it was amazing how they became one. Dusty never had to utter a verbal command; the wolf dog understood and obeyed the hand signals Dusty gave her.

Décor Photo, Wasilla, Alaska

As Dusty moved across the clearing on the blind side of the cabin, it flashed through his mind: anyone else could do the same. With a slight movement of Dusty's hand, Shadow Spirit dropped to the ground, muscles tense, ready to spring the moment any danger presented itself. Dusty stepped around the corner and silently onto the porch. He moved up to the window and carefully peered around the edge. Everything looked normal, but he still hesitated to call out Aura Lee's name. Through the window, the living room looked in order and he could even smell the fragrant aromas of Aura Lee's culinary expertise drifting from the kitchen. To the unsuspecting eye everything seemed normal, but to Dusty something was wrong ... terribly wrong!

Dusty moved to the door and with one smooth motion, he pulled back the hammer on his Winchester, and at a crouch, stepped through the door. Dusty could see the kitchen from the doorway and everything again looked normal. Dinner was in the middle of being prepared, but there was no Aura Lee to be found.

Décor Photo, Wasilla, Alaska

By now, close to panic, Dusty ran through the rest of the cabin shouting Aura Lee's name. When no reply came, he presumed the worst … someone had kidnapped his wife! Moving to the coat pegs beside the door to get his gun belt, he discovered his Colt missing from its holster. Believing the worst possible scenario, Dusty charged out the door calling the great white wolf dog into action.

"She's gone, girl! We've got ta find her! Find Aura Lee, Shadow Spirit, find her!"

At that command, Shadow Spirit sprung into action. It took only a moment to sniff the ground around the porch steps to pick up Aura

Lee's scent and with a shrill bark she bounded down the trail heading toward the creek.

At the cabin she had immediately picked up Aura Lee's scent and the new puppy's, but now as she headed down the creek trail she was getting another scent, one of another human, one she didn't recognize. For some reason unknown to Shadow Spirit this unfamiliar scent caused a renewed urgency and she picked up her pace. Dusty had a hard time keeping up with Shadow Spirit and had to stop and catch his breath every now and then. It was at one such stop that he took the time to closely examine the trail. Often the signs left by a person could tell a lot about him. That is if the person looking at the signs knew what he was doing.

Many a hard case was locked in the gray bar hotel who'd believed Dusty could track a honeybee through a meadow of wild flowers. When it came to tracking, not much got by Dusty's keen eyes. This time wasn't any different. Looking at the tracks was like reading a book to anyone else. The sign Dusty was studying brought a great deal of hope to him. By all indications Aura Lee hadn't been abducted, but instead was following someone and by the way it looked her new companion, Little Bear, was doing the tracking. The seriousness of the situation stopped Dusty from laughing, but the thought of that little ball of fur being anything other than a pet brought a slight smile to his face.

There was still plenty of light as Dusty started down the trail again at a ground-eating pace, but he knew nightfall wasn't far away and when it came, it came fast. He had to find Aura Lee before dark and hopefully before she caught up with whomever she was tracking.

Dusty had just slowed his pace because of several sharp turns in the trail, when he heard movement just a short distance ahead. Throwing caution to the wind he raced down the trail not knowing exactly what might be waiting for him, and to his surprise, as he rounded a bend he found himself looking down the barrel of a six-gun and it was rock steady.

≈ CHAPTER 9 ≈

*B*y now Aura Lee was too mad to feel much concern or fear for her safety. As she was heading back toward the cabin she realized her dinner was probably ruined, she looked a mess, and whatever or whoever was spying on her, had gotten away. When Little Bear, still in her arms, started growling as they were headed up the trail, she had just about enough. She ducked off the trail, and held her Colt cocked and ready.

Aura Lee wasn't sure who was more surprised, she or Dusty, when she stepped from behind a big cottonwood with the Colt held level and steady in one hand, and a ball of squirming white fur in the other.

"Easy, sweetheart ... How 'bout pointing that six-shooter some other direction than at my belly?"

Décor Photo, Wasilla, Alaska

Dusty tried to make light of the situation. "Look, if you're mad at me fer something, you didn't have ta run away from home! I'll apologize fer whatever I didn't know I did!"

"Oh' Dusty! You know I wasn't running away from home. Someone or something was sneaking around the cabin and before I could stop her, Little Bear was out the door and heading down the creek trail after whatever it was."

"Well, it looks to me you've gotten yerself a new, fierce protector there. What do ya think,

Shadow Spirit? ... Shadow Spirit? Shadow Spirit, come on, where did ya get ta?" Dusty suddenly realized the wolf dog wasn't in their midst.

All this time Dusty had thought she'd been tracking Aura Lee, but now he was beginning to rethink that. Maybe she was following the scent of whoever had been lurking about the cabin. This brought a moment of fear to Dusty and made the short hairs on the back of his neck stand up. Not wanting Aura Lee to worry, he covered his concern. "Come on, let's head back ta  the cabin. I'm sure Shadow Spirit will show up when she realizes she got on ta the wrong trail." Dusty tried to sound more confident than he was feeling. He knew Shadow Spirit was on the right trail as far as she was concerned, the trail of

Décor Photo, Wasilla, Alaska

danger, and even now she could be lying hurt somewhere along the way unconscious, or even worse, at the hands of the unseen menace who had been lurking outside their cabin.

Getting back to the cabin didn't seem to take near as long as it did to find Aura Lee. As the two broke into the clearing Aura Lee put Little Bear on the ground and the small white ball of fur bounded for the cabin. As soon as she reached the door she started to growl fiercely and bark in her puppy voice.

"Now what?" Dusty asked with an edge of agitation to his voice, more to himself than to Aura Lee. "You stay here till I have me a look inside. That sneakin' polecat you two were followin' mighta doubled back and be waitin' fer us."

Out of habit Dusty checked his Winchester to make sure a round was in the chamber, and then eased himself forward, keeping out of view of the front window. It was obvious to Dusty, because of the ruckus Little Bear was causing on the porch, that whoever was inside—if anybody—was forewarned, so the element of surprise was not in Dusty's favor. With these thoughts in mind, Dusty said to no one in particular, "Oh well," and he leaped to the porch, with his rifle at the ready. In an instant he was through the partially open door, ready for whatever consequence awaited him inside.

The jaunty little sea captain showed no alarm as Dusty came in a rush through the door with his rifle pointed in his direction.

"You sure have a strange way of welcoming an invited guest," Johnny said, with a grin on his face, nodding at Dusty's Winchester. "You did invite me to supper? When I got here the door was ajar so I let myself in. I didn't think you'd take offense to it."

By now Little Bear had made it into her old friend's lap, and Aura Lee, hearing friendly voices, had made her way to the cabin. When she entered, the captain politely stood, putting Little Bear on the floor, he greeted her with a, "Good evening ma'am, what ever you got cookin' in that kitchen of yours sure enough has my stomach a-yearnin' and a-growlin' like a hungry ole grizzly."

This brought a smile to Aura Lee's lips and lightened the moment, but the old sea captain knew something was amiss, and he knew Dusty would tell him what it was all about, so he paused to give Dusty a chance to speak.

Dusty got right into the subject by asking

Johnny if he'd noticed anyone lurking about when he came up to the cabin, and when the captain's answer was no, he went into detail about the events that had just taken place. When Dusty had finished, his friend began with a worried note to his voice …

"I knew when I laid eyes on some of my passengers comin' on board in Seattle, trouble was headin' north," his friend replied, sounding worried. The ones I have in mind didn't show up together. They kind of drifted on board at different times, and by the time we shoved off, I had counted nine mighty suspicious good-for-nothin's. I noticed they tried to act like they hadn't known each other before, but they weren't fooling anybody that was watching them closely."

Dusty nodded. "Sounds about right."

"That feller that calls himself Blackjack Jones, he's a curly, shifty no-count. Whenever I'd catch him talkin' to one of the others, he'd stop in mid-sentence and pretend like he didn't even know the other man was even standin' there. He made it a point, I'm sure, during the voyage to talk to each one of the nine when no one was around. That bunch is hatchin' somethin' and it won't amount to anythin' good, you can mark my words!"

As Dusty listened, his thoughts went to the letter in his pocket and then to the run-in he'd had with the Blackjack character earlier. Things were already starting to add up, and he didn't like the sum total so far.

While Dusty and the captain sat by the fire talking, Aura Lee excused herself and went to the kitchen to finish preparing dinner and set the table. As she went about this labor of love she hummed to herself one of her favorite hymns, *Rock of Ages.* They'd sung it practically every Sunday since the new parson, Reverend Blood, had started his church. To Aura Lee, singing always seemed to make things better, and right now she needed something to take her mind off whoever had been lurking around. She couldn't help wondering why anybody would be spying on them.

At dinner the conversation never turned to anything but friendly chatter and the catching up on the events of the past winter. Over generous slices of Aura Lee's dried apple pie and hot cups of coffee, Johnny told them he'd be leaving at the end of the week, on the morning tide.

In all the excitement and conversation no one had missed Shadow Spirit, but with the evening drawing to a close the captain asked, "Where's that ole wolf dog of yours? I haven't seen hide nor hair of her all night!"

Dusty explained about her taking to another trail, and he tried to make light of it, but Aura Lee could see the worry in his eyes, and she too was becoming concerned, for she had grown to love that big ole wolf dog almost as much as Dusty did.

Shadow Spirit had a sense about her that was hard to explain to people, but she could always tell when danger was near, be it man or animal. It wasn't like her to disappear when danger was afoot and there wasn't any doubt in Aura Lee's mind, danger was lurking very near.

It had grown late. Aura Lee insisted Johnny spend the night. After making him a pallet by the fireplace, and the good nights were said, the cabin soon became still. The only sound heard was the deep breathing of sleep.

CHAPTER 10

Dusty wasn't sure but his senses told him something was wrong. The cabin was cloaked in total darkness and not a sound could be heard. How long had he been asleep? What woke him up?

Slowly he eased out of bed and as he did so he felt a draft hit his bare feet—the door downstairs was open. He reached over to nudge Aura Lee awake and found her side of the bed empty.

Dusty slipped into his britches, pulled on his boots, and not making a sound, moved down the stairs. Stumbling over an unseen object on the floor caused Dusty to realize how strange it seemed to him that it would be so totally dark. It was summertime and he couldn't ever recall it being totally dark in the summer up here in Alaska. When he finally got a Lantern lit he was aghast at the disaster lying before him. Not a piece of furniture was left standing up-right. Dusty called out but no answer was forthcoming.

What had happened here? Where was Aura Lee or his friend Johnny Dynamite, and why hadn't he heard the noise this entire calamity would have caused?

"Shadow, Shadow Spirit!" Dusty called. He waited a moment for a response and then went to the kitchen only to find her sound asleep on the oval rug in front of the cookstove. This whole thing was getting stranger by the minute and Dusty was going to get to the bottom of it.

Strapping on his Colt he headed out the door with Shadow Spirit close behind. The wolf dog sensed the urgency in her master but acted like nothing was out of the ordinary. She didn't even seem to notice the disarray in the cabin as she passed through the greatroom going to the porch.

Outside the light was slightly better than in the cabin, but it was still strangely dark. Dusty wasn't sure what he was looking for or even why he had headed straight out the door. The only thing that was positive in his mind was that his wife and longtime friend were missing and by the looks of the cabin they hadn't gone willingly. While standing there in the darkness pondering the situation Dusty was alerted to a faint sound coming from the direction of the creek trail. He listened intently for a moment and there it was again—it sounded like a woman's scream and it sounded like Aura Lee! With long strides Dusty shot down the trail. After running for a time he could still hear the screams but it seemed like he wasn't getting closer. In his subconscious he felt something very wrong but couldn't put his finger on it. Stopping to catch his breath he noticed Shadow Spirit was missing. Not having the time or strength to wonder about it he lunged on, trying to catch up to his beloved wife before it was too late.

Now near exhaustion Dusty came to a bend in the trail and saw up ahead a slight glow flickering beyond the trees and he also noticed he could hear the screams more clearly. "I'm comin'," he shouted back, as best he could with what little breath he had left.

Charging into a clearing Dusty was momentarily dumbstruck. There before his eyes was his cabin and it was completely engulfed in flames. He could hear screams coming from within, but the fire was too hot for him to enter. Every time he made a charge for the door he was driven back by the flames until at last he collapsed to the ground in total exhaustion, and unable to move he cried out in anguish, "Aura Lee! Aura Lee! Aura Lee!"

Dusty slipped out of his exhausted sleep with soft, cool rain quietly falling on his face and on the cooling cabin fire. As he raised his head he could see the half-charred body of Shadow Spirit. The sight of the dead wolf dog brought Dusty sitting straight up. Then he remembered the fire and the screams. Aura Lee was gone and Shadow Spirit was dead too. She had died when she was overcome by fire and smoke trying to rescue Aura Lee.

Dusty's whole life had been in that fire. Everything he lived for had gone up in smoke. He was alone! What good would a marshal's badge do now? Along with Aura Lee and Shadow Spirit, those who broke the law had killed Dusty's will to go on. He was licked. Nothing else mattered. He didn't care. His strength left him and he fell face down in a patch of wet grass. As he lay in the wet grass he dreamed of his Andersonville Prison escape.

A young voice, filled with fear and excitement, shouted, "Here he is, I got him, I got him!"

The cold hand of fear gripped Dusty's heart as the young rebel's hand reached down and grabbed his arm. They had him. He fought and struggled but it was all in vain. There were too many and he was too exhausted to put up much of a fight. The rebel sergeant immediately pulled his pistol, laid it to Dusty's head, cocked the hammer back, and pulled the trigger.

In the split second before the gun went off Dusty looked up to see Sam and Blackjack holding cocked pistols to his head. "Good-bye Dusty Sourdough. You're off to the same place we sent your dogs and your women." Sam and Blackjack pulled the triggers at the same time.

Dusty could hear Aura Lee calling him. Her voice sounded like that of an angel. He heard the happy barks of Little Bear and Shadow Spirit. Dusty stood, and began to walk toward Aura Lee. Then he quickened his pace and they ran to meet each other. Dusty hugged Aura Lee over and over as Little Bear and Shadow Spirit barked their approval. They were all together again. Peace was surrounding them and their fight against evil had ended.

Dusty was a happy man.

The Adventures of Dusty Sourdough
by Glen Guy

THE ALASKA WILDERNESS SERIES

VISA   **MasterCard**

Please ship the following to:

First Name _____ Last Name _____

Mailing Address _____

City _____ State _____ Zip _____

Phone Number _____ Fax Number _____

☐Check ☐Money Order ☐VISA ☐M/C

Credit Card Number _____

Expiration Date _____ Signature _____

	Quantity	Total
A Gift for Dusty—Book 1 (Tenth Edition)	6.95 ea.	_____ $ _____
Dramatized Audio Tape (45 Minutes)	10.00 ea.	_____ $ _____
Trail to Wrangell—Book 2 (Third Edition)	9.95 ea.	_____ $ _____
Dramatized Audio Tape (Two Hours)	19.95 ea.	_____ $ _____
Gold—Book 3 (Second Edition)	9.95 ea.	_____ $ _____
Dramatized Audio Tape (Two Hours)	19.95 ea.	_____ $ _____
Fire—Book 4	9.95 ea.	_____ $ _____
Dramatized CD (Coming Soon)	19.95 ea.	_____ $ _____

Shipping and Handling. $ _____
First book S and H is $3. Other books on same order is $1 per book.

Grand Total $ _____

Please send orders to:
OLD ALASKA TODAY PUBLISHING
HC 33, Box 3191
Wasilla, Alaska 99654-9723
For Faster Service, Call Toll Free 1-877-935-7323
Email: oldalaskatoday@gci.net
Orders shipped via Priority Mail. Allow 10 days for delivery.